Cynthia DeFelice

Old Granny and the Bean Thief

Pictures by Cat Bowman Smith

FARRAR, STRAUS AND GIROUX

NEW YORK

To Grampy, an inspiration to us all
—C.D.

To Robert Trumbull Smith,
who knows about feisty grannies
—C.B.S.

Distributed in Canada by Douglas & McIntyre Ltd.
Color separations by Hong Kong Scanner Arts
Printed and bound in the United States of America by Berryville Graphics
Designed by Barbara Grzeslo
First edition, 2003
1 3 5 7 9 10 8 6 4 2

Library of Congress Cataloging-in-Publication Data
DeFelice, Cynthia C.
   Old Granny and the bean thief / Cynthia DeFelice ; pictures by
Cat Bowman Smith.
    p. cm.
   Summary: After a thief steals Old Granny's beans while she is asleep
at night, she gets some surprising help with catching him.
   ISBN 0-374-35614-9
   [1. Grandmothers—Fiction. 2. Beans—Fiction. 3. Robbers and
outlaws—Fiction. 4. Country life—Fiction.] I. Smith, Cat Bowman, ill.
II. Title.

PZ7.D3597 Ol 2003
[E]—dc21

                     2002020770

Old Granny loved beans. She always had beans in the oven, ready to eat whenever she felt like it, which was most of the time. She kept beans soaking in a pot of water, too, so they'd be soft and ready to cook.

Old Granny was lonely, living way out in the country with no one to talk to. She was happy enough, though, as long as she had her beans. But then one night a thief climbed through the window of her little cabin while she was sleeping. That thief ate up all the beans cooking in the oven, and all the beans soaking in the pot. And, as if that wasn't bad enough, he came back the next night and the night after that.

Old Granny was madder than a pussycat thrown into a pond. She was worried, too. What if he kept coming back night after night after night? Old Granny decided she'd better go to town to tell the sheriff about the bean thief.

It was a long way to town, so Old Granny got her walking stick and her sack and started out early. She hadn't gone very far before she came to a ditch. Old Granny didn't want to walk through it and get her feet all wet and muddy. She was about to jump over it when a water snake stuck its head up out of the water and spoke to her. "Hey, Old Granny!" it said. "Where are you going?"

Old Granny was a bit surprised, but she answered, "Three nights in a row, a thief has come sneaking into my cabin to steal my beans, and I'm going to tell the sheriff."

"Old Granny," said the snake, "on your way home, pick me up and put me in your sack. You'll be glad you did."

Old Granny thought that was pure nonsense. Why in thunder would she want to pick up a snake and put it in her sack? She flapped her hands and pulled her ear and said, "In a pig's eye! My, oh, my!" Then she went on her way.

Soon she was passing through a grove of pecan trees. A nut fell and landed at her feet. Old Granny was stepping around it when it spoke to her. "Hey, Old Granny! Where are you going?"

"Three nights in a row, a thief has come sneaking into my cabin to steal my beans, and I'm going to tell the sheriff," Old Granny answered.

"Old Granny," said the pecan, "on your way home, pick me up and put me in your sack. You'll be glad you did."

Old Granny thought that was downright silly. She flapped her hands and pulled her ear and said, "In a pig's eye! My, oh, my!" Then she went on her way.

Old Granny was walking along a road behind some cows. By and by, one of those cows stopped, lifted up its tail, and left a big old cow patty lying in the road.

Well, naturally, Old Granny didn't want to step in *that*. She was making her way around it when it spoke to her. "Hey, Old Granny! Where are you going?"

"Three nights in a row, a thief has come sneaking into my cabin to steal my beans, and I'm going to tell the sheriff," Old Granny answered.

"Old Granny," said the cow patty, "on your way home, pick me up and put me in your sack. You'll be glad you did."

Old Granny didn't think so, no sir. She flapped her hands and held her nose and said, "In a pig's eye! My, oh, my!" Then she went on her way.

Next, Old Granny came to a prickly pear cactus growing in the dust. She surely didn't want to step on it. As she started to walk by, the cactus spoke to her. "Hey, Old Granny! Where are you going?"

"Three nights in a row, a thief has come sneaking into my cabin to steal my beans, and I'm going to tell the sheriff," Old Granny answered.

"Old Granny," said the cactus, "on your way home, pick me up and put me in your sack. You'll be glad you did."

Old Granny flapped her hands and pulled her ear and said, "In a pig's eye! My, oh, my!" Then she went on her way.

Pretty soon she was close to town. She could see the sheriff's office on the other side of the river.

Crossing the bridge, she looked down at the water to see an alligator grinning at her, showing all its long, sharp teeth.

"Hey, Old Granny!" called the alligator. "Where are you going?"

"Three nights in a row, a thief has come sneaking into my cabin to steal my beans, and I'm going to tell the sheriff," Old Granny answered.

"Old Granny," said the alligator, "on your way home, pick me up and put me in your sack. You'll be glad you did."

Old Granny flapped her hands and pulled her ear and said, "In a pig's eye! My, oh, my!" Then she went on her way.

When Old Granny got to the sheriff's office, there was a sign on the door. *Gone Fishing*, it said.

What could Old Granny do? She turned around to start the
long walk home, feeling plumb discouraged and lonelier than ever.

As she walked across the bridge, she saw the alligator grinning and waving cheerfully. Old Granny was so glad to see a friendly face that she picked up the alligator and put it in her sack. "After all," she told herself, "it spoke to me quite politely."

The prickly pear cactus was still growing in the dust, waiting for her. So she picked up that cactus real careful-like and put it in her sack. "After all," she said, "it will be pleasant to have some company around the house."

As she walked down the road, Old Granny remembered what she'd seen there before. She surely hoped it wouldn't be there anymore.

But it was.

Old Granny wanted to walk right on by, but that hardly seemed sociable. "Besides," she had to admit, "it isn't every day you see a talking cow patty." So Old Granny took a deep breath, picked up the cow patty, and put it in her sack.

Soon she came to the pecan. She thought she might ignore it, but that didn't seem fair. "After all, what harm could there be in picking up a tiny nut?" she thought. She stopped and put it in her sack.

When Old Granny was almost home, she came to the ditch, where the water snake was waiting for her, flashing its pointy tongue. She couldn't pass it by. "After all," she told herself, "it was the first thing to speak to me in a long, long time." So she picked up the snake, put it in her sack, and went on her way.

When she got home, Old Granny emptied her sack and said, "Where in the world will I put you all?"

The alligator spoke up first. "Put me in the pond out in your yard, Old Granny."

That made sense to Old Granny, so that was just what she did.

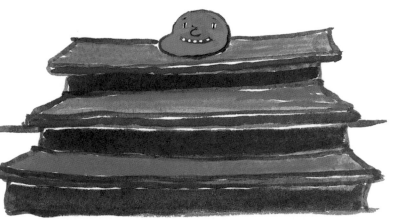

The prickly pear cactus said, "Old Granny, see those three steps going up to your little cabin? Plant me in the dust at the bottom of the steps."

So she did.

The cow patty said, "Old Granny, put me right in the middle of the top step."

So she did.

The pecan said, "Old Granny, put me in the oven with the beans you've got cooking there."

So she did.

The water snake said, "Old Granny, put me right in that pot of water where you're soaking your beans."

So she did.

Old Granny was tired and hungry from walking all the way to town and back, carrying her sack. She ate some beans, said good night to her new friends, got into bed, and was asleep almost the instant her head touched the pillow.

Old Granny was snoring away in her bed when that bean thief came sneaking back into her cabin. He knew just what he wanted, and he knew where it was, too, on account of being there three times before.

He headed straight for the pot of water where the beans were soaking. He took off the lid, got up on his tippy-toes, and reached way down into the pot to grab a handful of beans.

Out of the pot rose the snake, hissing and flashing its pointy tongue. "Yeee-oow!" shouted the thief.

He was about to run for the door when he smelled the beans cooking, and he just had to have some. Now, the pecan had been sitting in that oven for a long time, and it was hot. When the thief reached into the oven, the nut popped right out and hit him smack in the eye.

"Yeee-oow!" shouted the thief.

He ran out the door, hit the top step, slipped on the cow patty, lost his balance, and went head over heels to the bottom of the steps . . .

. . . where he landed on *his* bottom, right on the prickly pear cactus.

"Yeee-oow!" shouted the thief.

He was running away just as fast as he could when he looked down at his foot. "Ewww, yuck!"

Then he saw the pond and said, "Good! I can go over there and wash this stuff off." He stuck his foot into the water to rinse it off, and "Yeee-oow!" the alligator bit him.

His last shout woke up Old Granny. She got her stick and started chasing after him. "Stop, thief! Stop, thief! Stop, thief!"

The snake, the pecan, the cow patty, the prickly pear cactus, and the alligator hollered, too: "Stop, thief! Stop, thief! Stop, thief!"

They scared the thief so badly he never dared to go near Old Granny's cabin again. Old Granny is still living there, happily talking with her friends and eating beans.

And that's the truth. If you don't believe it, just ask the cow patty.